IS BLOOMSBURY BOOK

BELONGS TO

. . . .

T
o

Bloomsbury Publishing, London, Berlin and New York

First published in Great Britain in 2008 by Bloomsbury Publishing Plc
36 Soho Square, London, W1D 3QY

This paperback edition first published in 2009

Audio copyright in recording © and ℗ Bloomsbury Publishing Plc 2008
Music composed by Andy Quin and licensed by MPCS on behalf of De Wolfe Music

A CIP catalogue record of this book is available from the British Library

ISBN 978 0 7475 9524 3

Printed in China

1 3 5 7 9 10 8 6 4 2

FSC
Mixed Sources
Product group from well-managed
forests and other controlled sources
Cert no. SCS-COC-00927
www.fsc.org
© 1996 Forest Stewardship Council

www.bloomsbury.com/childrens
www.bloomsbury.com/animalantics

The Selfish Crocodile

Book of

Nursery Rhymes

Faustin Charles

Illustrated by
Michael Terry

BLOOMSBURY

LONDON BERLIN NEW YORK

Rock-a-bye birdie on the treetop,
When the wind blows the nest will rock;

When the branch breaks the nest will fall,
And down will come birdie, nest and all.

Little bird blue, come sing your song,
The chicks in the nest aren't very strong.
Where is the mummy who looks after their keep?
She's under the tree there, fast asleep!

One, two, three, four, five,

Once I caught a snake alive;

Six, seven, eight, nine, ten,

Then I let it go again.

Why did you let it go?

Because it bit my little toe.

Which toe did it bite?

This little red one on the right.

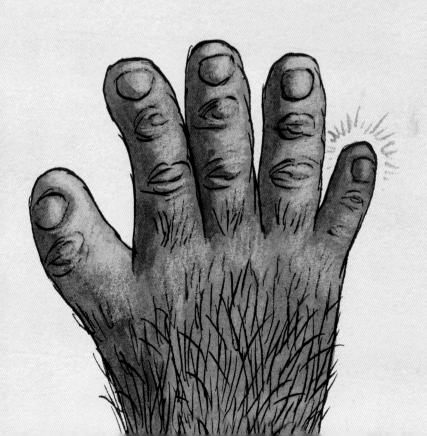

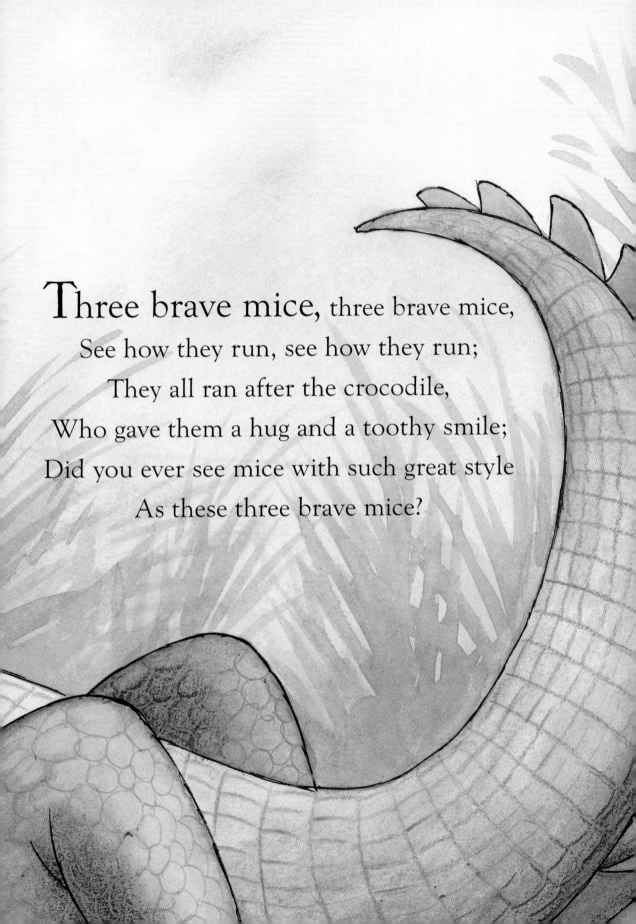

Three brave mice, three brave mice,
See how they run, see how they run;
They all ran after the crocodile,
Who gave them a hug and a toothy smile;
Did you ever see mice with such great style
As these three brave mice?

Little Zack Zebra

Stood by the river,

Eating the grass nearby.

He put out his tongue,

Then spat out a plum,

And said,
"What a good zebra am I!"

The racing wild deer ran down to the river
In a shower of rain.
He slipped on a stone, almost breaking a bone,
And never went down there again.

Zippy, Zippy, the greedy zebra,
Had a calf and couldn't keep her;
She put her in a tortoise shell
And there she kept her very well.

Chicks and cubs, come out to play,
The sun is shining every day;
Leave the nests and leave the pride,
And join us by the riverside.

Come with a swoop, come with a call,
Come with a cheer or not at all;
From the trees and from the ground,
We are waiting to hear the sound.

There was
an old lion
Who lived under a hill,
And if he's not gone,
He lives there still.

I love little squirrel, his fur is so warm,

And if I don't hurt him, he'll do me no harm;

I'll not pull his tail, nor chase him away,

And squirrel and I will play gently all day.

Ding, dong, yell,
Leopard slipped and fell.
Who helped her up?
The monkey with a stick.
Who said hello?
Little baby hippo.

Who began to laugh?
It was the baby calf.
What a naughty calf was that
To make fun of leopard lying flat,
Who never called him nasty names,
But played in all his riverside games.

Dickory, dickory, dock,

A bird flew from a flock.

The flock circled round

As he flapped to the ground,

Dickory, dickory, dock.

Twinkle, twinkle, butterfly,

How I wonder where you fly,

Up above the trees so high,

Like a sunbeam in the sky.

Twinkle, twinkle, butterfly,

How I wonder where you fly.

I had a
little fruit tree,
Nothing would it bear,
But a single nut
And an avocado pear.
The crocodile's big brother
Came to visit me,
All because of my
Little fruit tree.

Crocodile, crocodile,
where have you been?
I've been where crocodiles
haven't been seen.

Crocodile, crocodile,
what did you there?
I saved a mouse
from a lion's lair.

Elephant be nimble,
Elephant be quick,

Elephant jumps over
A long brown stick.

Teeth, teeth, shining bright,

Even in the darkest night.

Teeth, teeth, sharp and strong,

Teeth, teeth, white and long.

There was an old lioness who lived in a zoo,
She wanted to get out but she didn't know how to;
She was given some broth and some stale brown bread,
She lay in the cage and pretended to be dead.

High-uppity giraffe standing tall,
High-uppity giraffe had a great fall;

All the big cats from the lion's den
Couldn't make giraffe stand up straight again.

Come and bathe in the river,

Come and have a nice drink,

Come and swim in the river,

But be careful not to sink.

Baby gorilla
sitting in a tree,
Baby gorilla
scratching
his fleas,

Baby gorilla
holding
on to Mummy,
Baby gorilla
rubbing
his tummy.

The mouse and the crocodile

Went on holiday,

Quite where to they didn't say;

They brought back strawberries,

Sweet plum and cherries,

And a giant nut wrapped up in hay.

The crocodile's teeth go

CRUNCH, CRUNCH, CRUNCH,

Whenever he's having fruit for lunch.

Sitting by the river with such a big smile,

He's no longer a selfish crocodile.

The mouse and the crocodile

Went to the river

To get a drink of water;

The mouse fell down
And almost drowned,
But the crocodile went in after.

A crayfish

climbing a tree

Is the funniest thing

you'll ever see.

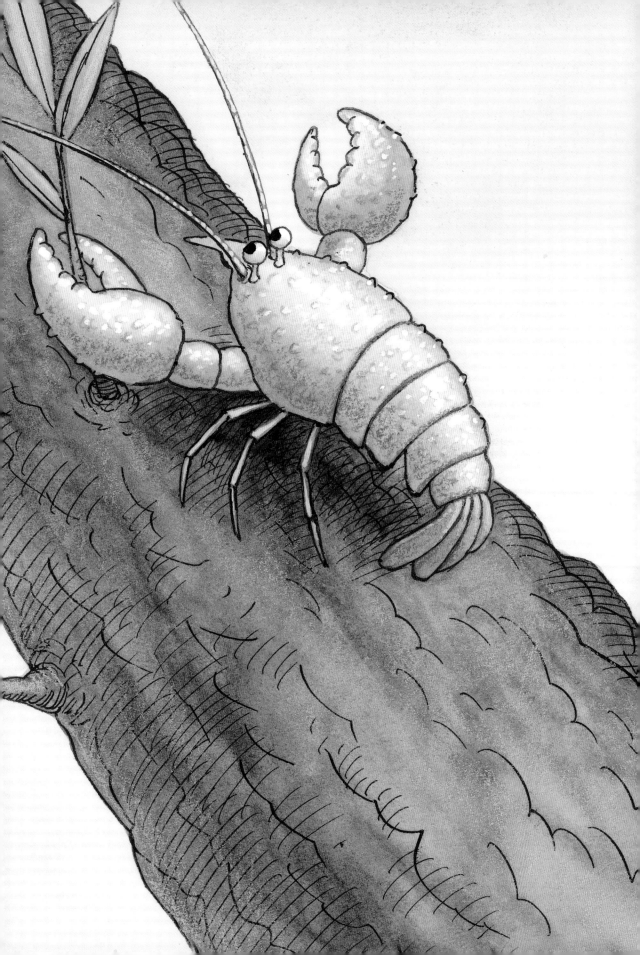

Hey diddle, diddle,

The mouse in a puddle,

The crocodile jumped over the moon;

The green frog
laughed to see such fun,

And a fish swam away with a baboon.

Little alligator
Yelled for his supper.

What shall he eat?
Berries and banana.
What shall he drink?
Warm river water.

Sing a song of birdsongs,
Hear the eagles cry,
Four-and-twenty blackbirds
High in the sky.

The sky was blue and sunny,

The birds began to play;

Wasn't that a dainty song

To brighten up the day?

The lion was in the forest,
Chasing away a monkey.
The lioness was by the river,
Eating nuts and honey.

The zebra was in the meadow,
Admiring her toes,
When down flew a little bird
And pecked her on the nose!

Bumble bee, bumble bee,

Have you any honey?

Buzz, buzz, monkey, I have plenty.

Some for the squirrel and the alligator,

And some for the deer

drinking in the river.

This little wild pig
went in the river,

This little wild pig
stayed by Mother,

This little wild pig
had a juicy ripe plum,

This little wild pig
had none,

And this little wild pig cried,
"I want some!"

Monkey had a little bird,
Its feathers were like a rainbow,
And everywhere that monkey went
The bird was sure to follow.

Little Miss Zebra

Sat by the river,
Chewing her curds and hay;
Along came an alligator,
Who sat down beside her
And frightened Miss Zebra away!

Go to sleep, baby raccoon,
Daddy will be home soon,
Bringing a piece of juicy plum
To give his raccoon baby some.

Enjoy more animal antics from
Faustin Charles & Michael Terry . . .

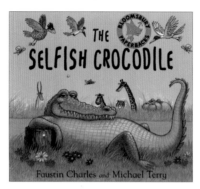

The Selfish Crocodile
by Faustin Charles
& illustrated by Michael Terry

The Lonely Giraffe
by Peter Blight
& illustrated by Michael Terry

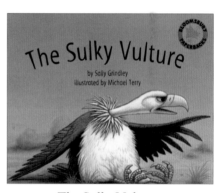

The Sulky Vulture
by Sally Grindley
& illustrated by Michael Terry

The Gossipy Parrot
by Shen Roddie
& illustrated by Michael Terry

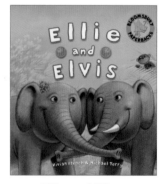

Ellie and Elvis
by Vivian French
& illustrated by Michael Terry